The Night Before CHRISTMAS

Sue Carabine

Illustrations by

Shauna Mooney Kawasaki

GIBBS SMITH
TO ENRICH AND INSPIRE HUMANKIND

Salt Lake City | Charleston | Santa Fe | Santa Barbara

13 12 11 10   9 8 7 6

Published by
Gibbs Smith
P.O. Box 667
Layton, Utah 84041

1.800.835.4993 orders
www.gibbs-smith.com

Designed and produced by TTA Design
Printed and bound in China
Gibbs Smith books are printed on either recycled,
100% post-consumer waste, FSC-certified papers
or on paper produced from a 100% certified sus-
tainable forest / controlled wood source.

ISBN 13: 978-1-58685-276-4
ISBN 10: 1-58685-276-0

'Twas the night before Christmas
on this snowy white day,
Nick was feeling quite pleased
as they flew on their way.

When, suddenly, one of the
sleigh's runners came loose,
He called to his deer,
"I must tighten the screws!"

He whistled instructions
as they dashed toward the ground,
But the parking was hopeless,
not a spot could be found.

"Whoa, there," Nick cried
in a sharp urgent tone,
And he directed the sleigh
to a 'No Parking' zone.

"We need a screwdriver
to get on our way,
Come on, boys, let's find one!
We must not delay!"

They knew that the runner
must quickly be mended,
So they covered the toys,
left the sleigh unattended.

Two highway patrolmen
came cruising along
And spotting the sleigh,
they knew something was wrong.

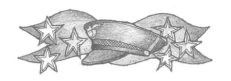

One officer circled it,
looked for its owner,
Uncovered the back space.
The toys made him wonder,

"Now, who could have left
all these things to be stolen?"
And, shaking his head,
called the other patrolman.

(Then, what followed next
wouldn't have happened that day
Had they known the contraption
was St. Nicholas's sleigh.)

The officers impounded
the sleigh with its load,
Then, ending their shift,
they both headed for home.

Dear Santa, meanwhile,
with his reindeer in tow,
Purchased the tool and called,
"Come, boys, let's go!"

But they were dismayed
when they all arrived back
And saw the sleigh missing,
along with Nick's sack.

"Now, who could have done this?
Where can it have gone?
Call the finest for help, boys!
Quick! Dial 9-1-1!"

On hearing the call,
the dispatcher looked grim,
And immediately put out
an All Points Bulletin!

Before Santa knew it,
the police came along,
So eager to right
this most terrible wrong.

While Nick and his reindeer
went down to the station,
To answer some questions
(they tried to be patient),

All law enforcement,
along with their hounds,
Searched for the packed sleigh
for many miles 'round.

Detectives stood ready,
dropped all other cases,
A look of resolve
upon each of their faces.

Their own kids at home
were awaiting Nick's call,
If he didn't show,
their sweet faces would fall.

So they called all their contacts
and even their snitchers,
Dragged some to the station
to go through mug pictures!

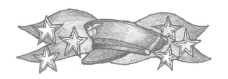

Now, two more policemen
were out on their beat,
Keeping neighborhoods safe
by patrolling the streets.

They answered the call
just as soon as they heard,
Said, "Stealing Nick's sleigh,
now that is absurd!"

They carefully covered
all six housing floors
When finally they knocked
on the building's last door.

Two very small children
said, "May we help you?"
The officers asked,
"Is your mommy here too?"

Said nine-year-old Steven,
with a sad little grin,
"Our mama is sick.
Would you like to come in?"

The officers entered and
with care looked around.
But no tree or gifts in
this home could be found.

"This is no way to spend Christmas," they whispered. "We must do something special for him and his sister!"

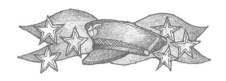

They decided right then
to make a few calls,
And bring joy, gifts, and Christmas
to those sorrowful walls.

Then they continued
their search for the sleigh.
Determined to find it,
they vowed, "Come what may."

When news reached the ears
of the motorbike cops,
They also decided
to pull out all stops.

They'd be on the job
for the rest of the night
(Only Santa could fill
their kids' hearts with delight).

They too tried to locate
St. Nicholas's sleigh,
To bring joy to children
on this Christmas Day.

In fact, all departments
from bottom to top
Were doing their best,
even tired traffic cops.

As they checked each stopped car,
they went out of their way,
But no one could find
old St. Nicholas's sleigh.

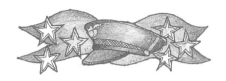

Two highway patrolmen
pulled over a car
That was traveling way over
the limit, by far.

As the vehicle stopped
and the patrolmen approached,
A young man yelled out,
"Just slow down, I'm your coach!"

They took in the scene
and thought, "This guy is crazy!"
Then realized his young wife
was having a baby!

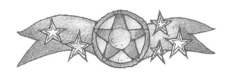

"Let us help you," they urged,
"we have done this before,"
And an officer climbed in
when he opened the door.

Soon a sweet cry was heard,
one that we all know,
And a new babe was born,
just like long, long ago!

From detective to sergeant
to captain to mayor,
Why, even the President
applied his own pressure:

He called Santa Claus
and promised him true,
"I'm sending the
FBI, CIA, too!"

Nick kindly said, "Thank you,
now that's quite a feat.
But the police here are super,
they don't miss a beat!

He hung up the phone
to the officers' applause,
Who cheered, "You're our
honorary Officer Claus!"

In one Yule-lit home,
children woke up their dad,
Crying, "Something has happened!
It's awful, it's bad!

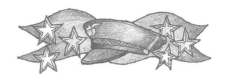

"Santa's sleigh has gone missing,
and now he can't come."
Then the horrified officer
knew what he had done!

He called up the station,
feeling sick deep inside,
But when Santa Claus heard,
he just laughed till he cried!

"You were doing your job, son,
you're a good honest man,
But now we must leave
to do ours, if we can!"

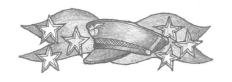

And so on this beautiful,
calm Christmas Eve,
Bundled up in his sleigh,
Nick was ready to leave.

He thanked them and said,
"You're the finest police,
May Christmas fill all of
your hearts with great peace!"